How Can I Help, Papa?

A Child's Journey Through Loss and Healing

Written by **Elissa Al-Chokhachy**

Illustrated by **Ulrike Graf**

This is a story about my Papa, the best grandfather in the whole world. When I was little, my mother and I visited Papa often. He greeted us at the front door smiling. "Glad to see you, Pumpkin," he'd say in his deep loud voice. I'd give him a kiss on the cheek. Papa would tickle me when I reached up my arms to give him a hug.

We played games like Hide-and-Go-Seek, Trot, Trot to Boston, or his own unique game called "I'm gonna get you!" Papa would chase me, saying "I'm gonna get you!" I would run as fast as I could to try to get away. When Papa caught me, he'd tickle me and I'd laugh so hard tears would run down my cheeks.

Papa knew how to make me laugh. He was silly, so I'd be silly. I couldn't help it. It was so much fun!

One day when I was nine years old, I came home from school to find Momma crying. "What's wrong?" I asked.

"Papa's very sick," she said sadly.

"Is he going to get better?"

"I don't know, Pumpkin. I hope so, but I just don't know." Momma hugged me. I felt her wet tears on my face. I cried too.

The next day we visited Papa. He smiled when I saw him. "Glad to see you, Pumpkin," he said. When I wrapped my arms around his neck, Papa only tickled me a little. That day Papa stayed in his chair the whole time. When I asked if he would come out to play, he said, "I'm sorry. I can't chase you, Pumpkin. I'm not feeling strong today."

"That's okay," I said. But it really wasn't. I was mad. It wasn't fair. I went outside alone that day. "Take that!" I said under my breath to the soccer ball as I kicked it against the wall. "It's just not fair!" Somehow it helped to kick the ball that day. It couldn't make Papa better though. That night, before I went to sleep, I prayed that Papa would get better.

Each time we visited, Papa always welcomed me with a smile. But he seemed weaker. I didn't know what to do. One day I asked, "How can I help you, Papa?"
"You can sit here and keep me company," he said, patting the sofa next to him. "That would make me feel better."

And so I did. Each time we visited, I kept my Papa company. "How can I help, Papa?" I asked. Sometimes he wanted me to get him a drink of water or a snack. Other times he'd have me scratch his back. Of course, if I scratched his back, I would have to tickle him. Sometimes it made him laugh.

"Tell me about school, Pumpkin," he would say. I shared stories, especially the funny ones. I made him pictures and "I love you, Papa" cards which he hung proudly on his refrigerator door. "Thank you, Pumpkin," he'd say. It felt good to do nice things for Papa.

One day, while I was sitting with him, I got sad. "Are you going to get better, Papa?" I asked.

"I don't know, Pumpkin," he said. Tears were in Papa's eyes. "The doctors tell me I am very sick. They don't think I'm going to get better. But I know it's important not to give up hope."

"I don't want you to be sick, Papa," I said, starting to cry. "I love you."

"I know you do, Pumpkin. I love you too. But if my time has come, it will be okay. Everything changes. Nothing stays the same. Every year the seasons come and go. Pumpkin, it's important to make the most of what we have today."

That day, no matter what my Papa said, I couldn't stop crying. So Papa put his arm around me and held me until I felt better. "But if you don't get better, Papa, it won't be the same."

"You're right. It never is." He took a deep breath and paused.

"When Nana died, it was really hard for me because I missed her so much. I remembered my mother teaching me that whenever God closes a door, He always opens a window. Every day I prayed for strength and courage. And as time went on, life got easier. I learned how to live differently. Then you came into my life." Papa smiled. "Now I can't imagine life without my Pumpkin."

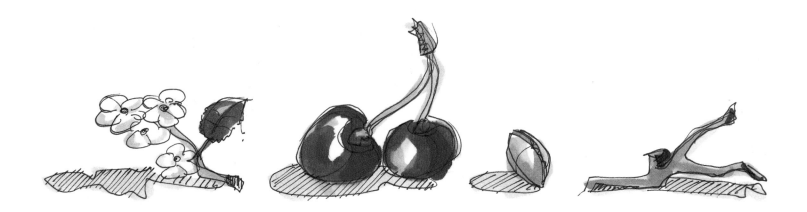

"I still miss Nana. I loved her with all my heart. I still do. Remember, Pumpkin, love never dies. Someday I hope Nana and I will be together again.

"When you think of me, smile. Remember all the good times we've had and everything we've shared. Know that I will always love you.

"It's okay to feel sad, Pumpkin. But also be glad. I've had a good life. I did all the things I wanted to do. I married a wonderful woman, had a beautiful daughter and a beautiful granddaughter. And many, many years from now, we'll all be together again.

"Whatever you do, I want you to remember to always follow your heart. Choose the friends and things that make you the happiest. It helped me live a full life. I want the same for you."

"Thanks, Papa."

The next time I visited his home, I was surprised to find Papa propped up in a strange-looking bed in the middle of the living room. "Why are you in a bed, Papa?" I asked. "And where's your bed?"

"It's okay, Pumpkin. Don't be frightened. This is a hospital bed," he explained. "It makes it easier for me to sit up. And sitting up helps me breathe better too."

"Ohhhhh," I said, feeling somewhat relieved. Still concerned, I asked quietly, "How can I help you today, Papa?"
"Sit and spend time with me like you always do," he said softly. "It makes me happy."
"I'm glad, Papa. It makes me happy too."

From then on, we visited Papa every day. Momma wanted to take Papa to our home to take care of him. But Papa wanted to stay in the same house that he and Nana had shared for forty years. So, Momma hired a nice nurse to care for Papa during the time we couldn't be there.

On our next visit, the nurse was taking care of Papa. She told us he was much weaker now and only able to eat a little. We could offer him something but it was important not to force him if he didn't feel like eating or drinking.

Then Papa started talking out loud. "You're waiting for me, Nana? Everything's all set?"

The nurse said, "Often people in the last weeks of life have visions of loved ones who have died. Perhaps Papa can see and hear things we aren't able to see and hear. It is important to honor Papa and his experience."

I wished I could see Nana too.

Since Papa was sleeping most of the time, I missed our talks. The nurse explained that although Papa's medicine took away his pain, it sometimes made him sleepy. Momma and I were glad to know that at least Papa was comfortable.

I asked the nurse how I could help Papa if he's sleeping all the time. She suggested that I sit and hold his hand. I could talk to Papa about things we had done together. He would know I was there. I could also play his favorite music. Papa would hear.

And that's what I did. Each time we visited, I sat and held my Papa's hand. Sometimes I talked. Other times I played his favorite songs. It felt good to be able to do something for him. I loved Papa. I still do.

The last day I saw Papa was the hardest day of all. The nurse called us to come say goodbye. When we got there, she said, "Papa is very sick. It won't be long now. It may be hard for Papa because a part of him wants to stay here with you and Momma. He loves you. But he can't stay. His body is tired. It doesn't work the way it use to.

"There are things you can say that may help Papa come to a place of peace. Although he can't talk to you, Papa does hear everything you say. Let him know you'll take care of each other. And if you are able, let him know it's okay if he's ready to let go.

"Thank him for everything he's done for you. If there's something that you feel bad about, remember, it's never too late to say 'I'm sorry.' Most of all, tell Papa how much you love him and always will."

I asked him, "How can I help you, Papa?" He didn't answer. In my heart, I knew the answer. I didn't want to say goodbye, but I didn't want it to be hard for Papa.

"Papa, I love you," I said with tears in my eyes. "If you have to go to Heaven, it's okay. Nana's waiting for you. Momma and I will be all right. We'll look after each other. Thanks for being the best Papa in the whole world."

Momma said goodbye too. We cried and hugged each other. The nurse hugged us both. It was the hardest thing I ever did. But I was glad I did everything I could for Papa.

That night Papa died peacefully in his sleep. I know he went to Heaven. Life is different now. It's been two years since he died. At first I cried a lot. I didn't think I would stop. But pretty soon I did. I still miss Papa. Sometimes I write him a letter. Here's the last one I wrote:

Dear Papa,

How's Heaven? Do you like it? How's Nana? I bet you guys are having a wonderful time up there. Did you meet God? What's He like? Have you seen any angels? I still miss you, Papa.

Someday, when I grow older, I'll play the same games with my children that you played with me. I'll tell them about my Papa, the best grandfather in the whole wide world! I'm glad we got to spend time together. I'm glad I was able to help. I love you, Papa!

With love forever and ever,

Pumpkin

P.S. Remember how you said to always follow my heart? I am. Maggie's now my best friend and I love playing soccer. You're the best, Papa!

Published in the
United States of America by
Works of Hope Publishing
149 Eastern Avenue
Gloucester, MA 01930
Printed in Singapore.
Book design by
Vail Edward Walter.

Library of Congress
Cataloging-in-Publication Data
Al-Chokhachy, Elissa.
How can I help, Papa? :
a child's journey through
loss & healing / written by
Elissa Al-Chokhachy ;
illustrated by Ulrike Graf.
--1st ed, p. cm.

ISBN: 0-9712481-0-9
SUMMARY: A girl describes
her relationship with her
grandfather, and how
she dealt with his
approaching death.

1. Terminally ill–Family relationships
—Juvenile fiction.
2. Grandfathers—Juvenile fiction.
3. Death—Juvenile fiction.
[1. Terminally ill—Fiction.
2. Grandfathers—Fiction.
3. Death—Fiction.]
I. Graf, Ulrike, 1973- II. Title.
PZ7.A328How 2002 [E] QBI01-201125